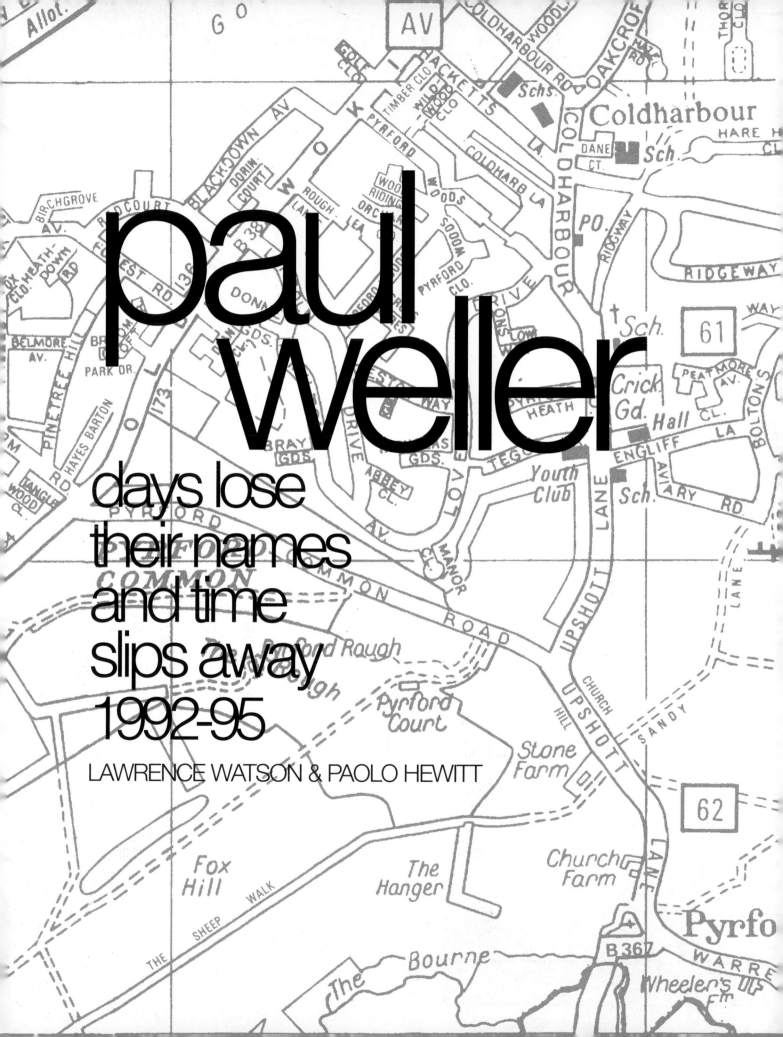

paul weller

days lose their names and time slips away 1992-95

LAWRENCE WATSON & PAOLO HEWITT

PAUL WELLER DEDICATES THIS BOOK TO ROAD CREWS AND TOUR MANAGERS EVERYWHERE.

LAWRENCE WATSON DEDICATES THIS BOOK TO SHARON, TRAVIS AND MILES.

FIRST PUBLISHED IN THE UK IN 1995 BY
BOXTREE LIMITED
BROADWALL HOUSE
21 BROADWALL
LONDON SE1 9PL

IN ASSOCIATION WITH GO! DISCS
72 BLACK LION LANE
HAMMERSMITH
LONDON W6 9BE

BOOK DESIGN BY SIMON HALFON, THREE LIONS D.A. AND KEN DAVIS

PRINTED AND BOUND IN GREAT BRITAIN BY CAMBUS LITHO, EAST KILBRIDE

ISBN 0 7522 0754 7 PAPERBACK
ISBN 0 7522 0235 9 LIMITED EDITION HARDBACK

A CATALOGUE ENTRY FOR THIS BOOK IS AVAILABLE FROM THE BRITISH LIBRARY

SPECIAL THANKS GO TO PAUL WELLER'S ROAD CREW, ALL AT SOLID BOND AND EVERYONE AT GO! DISCS, ESPECIALLY
PETER MASON, MARILYN FIRTH AND MICHELLE POTTER. MANY THANKS ALSO TO JAKE LINGWOOD AT BOXTREE.

WHEN I WAS 12 OR COMING ON 13, MY DAD BOUGHT ME AN ELECTRIC GUITAR. WE DIDN'T KNOW ABOUT AMPLIFIERS UNTIL A LOT LATER. I GOT RIGHT INTO IT. I LOVED IT AND CHERISHED IT. I EVEN SLEPT WITH IT ON TOP OF MY BED. I LOOKED INTO MY MAGIC MIRROR EVERY NOW AND THEN, TRYING TO SEE IF I HAD GOT "IT" YET. AFTER THAT PERIOD I SET ABOUT ACTUALLY LEARNING IT. A BAND GOT FORMED. WE REHEARSED IN MY BEDROOM AT STANLEY ROAD FOR 3/4 NIGHTS A WEEK UNTIL WE WERE GOOD ENOUGH TO GO OUT TO PLAY TO PEOPLE AND GET PAID. WE WERE A GROUP.

A HUNDRED YEARS LATER I WOKE UP IN 1990 WITHOUT A DEAL, A RECORDING OR PUBLISHING CONTRACT, WITHOUT A GROUP, WITHOUT A BASE. THE EVIL CURSE HAD ENDED OR THE BEAUTIFUL DREAM HAD JUST BEGUN. AND THERE WAS STILL TWO OF US. WITHOUT POINT OR REASON, I CO-PRODUCED AN ALBUM WITH MY WIFE DEE C. LEE AND DR. ROBERT. NOTHING HAPPENED. I WENT ON TOUR. NOTHING HAPPENED. A YEAR LATER ME AND MC LYNCH OF SOLID BOND STUDIOS PUT A TRACK TOGETHER IN THE BACK-ROOM (WHILST THE YOUNG DISCIPLES FINISHED "ROAD TO FREEDOM" IN THE MAIN STUDIO).

WE RELEASED THIS TRACK ON OUR OWN SOLID BOND FINANCED LABEL, "FREEDOM HIGH". IT GOT TO NO. 37 OR SOMETHING BUT MOST IMPORTANTLY IT WAS A BOSS RECORD AND MADE ME AND ALL OF US (THE SOLID BOND TEAM) THINK IT WAS WORTH GOING ON. AND WE DID.

IN '91/'92, I TOURED FAIRLY CONSISTENTLY. IN THE SHEFFIELD OCTAGON THERE WAS A SMALL CROWD. IN MANCHESTER ACADEMY, A FULL HOUSE. IT VARIED. PEOPLE WERE IN TWO MINDS. SO WERE MY FRIENDS AND FAMILY. SO WAS I. I STILL AM BUT I TELL YOU WHAT, FAIR DROOGS, I'VE CHECKED WHAT MARVIN G. SAID IN THAT BELGIUM DOCUMENTARY. HE SAID, "NO ONE CAN TAKE AWAY MY TALENT." MY PARAPHRASE BUT I DIG IT. THAT'S WHAT I KNOW. I *CAN* PLAY GUITAR. I *CAN* SING. I *CAN* WRITE AND I *CAN* REACH PEOPLE. WE ALL MESS UP (IF WE'RE LUCKY) BUT DON'T ANYONE EVER DETER YOU FROM YOUR THING, *YOUR* DREAM. TAKE IT TO THE HILT, YOU CAN ONLY FAIL. SOMETIMES YOU CAN SAIL.

PAUL WELLER, MAY 1995.

San Francisco, March 1993

To go on tour is to enter a bubble where the days lose their names and time slips away. In that bubble nothing matters except one thing: that night's concert. From the minute your eyes flutter open like butterflies struggling to fly, all the way to close down, that is all you are concerned with; that night's concert.

Paul's shows followed a distinct pattern. Little was said on stage. It was implied that the music would do all the communicating. This is how it should be and this is where Paul and his band had to be on top. Music was their language and the means of communication was mostly in their hands.

lost nights they
succeeded because it
was here, under the
boiling lights, the eyes
of that night's world
upon them, that they
so obviously belonged.
And because of that,
because of this commit-
ment, this was the point
where the music would
take on a life of its own,
where it would charge
you and take over,
where it would dip and
change colours, rush
towards and then
swerve sideways for a
brief resting place,
before carrying on this
magical journey to the
heights, the place where
we all want to be.

And it was in that
sound that you would
hear all the emotions
that living in the bubble
demands of you. The
stale time of the dressing
room, those hours
before the gig which
pass so slowly. The
noise as the lights finally dimmed, the quiet
hours on the coach
watching the road speed
by, the intense conver-
sations and the lonely
smell of unfamiliar
hotel rooms. The ever-
present tiredness that
you wore every day and
the longing for those
moments, sudden
unexpected moments in
roadside cafés or hotel
lobbies, that would
crack open the pressure
valve and let you
breathe again.

And as all those
feelings, those strange
feelings, hit you and
changed you and made
you see parts of yourself
and others that you
never knew existed,
somehow they all built
to that magical moment
when the band were on
stage and the audience
was in sync and the
value of music, this
God-given thing that we
gladly give our lives
over to, was reinforced
and reinstated and
made safe and sure in
our heads again.

And at the end of it all,
as you waved goodbye
to all those concert
halls and venues like
loved ones departing,
you would come blink-
ing out of the bubble
and know that you
would have to change
again to meet the world
and all of its demands.
But by then it was too
late. The memories were
etched far too deep and
so was the feeling.

What do you get from the following Lennon quote:
"I always thought that about myself.
Half of me thinks I'm a loser and the other half thinks I'm God almighty."

*"It's how I always felt, even at school, but I couldn't take myself that seriously.
I've always thought I'm just lucky."*

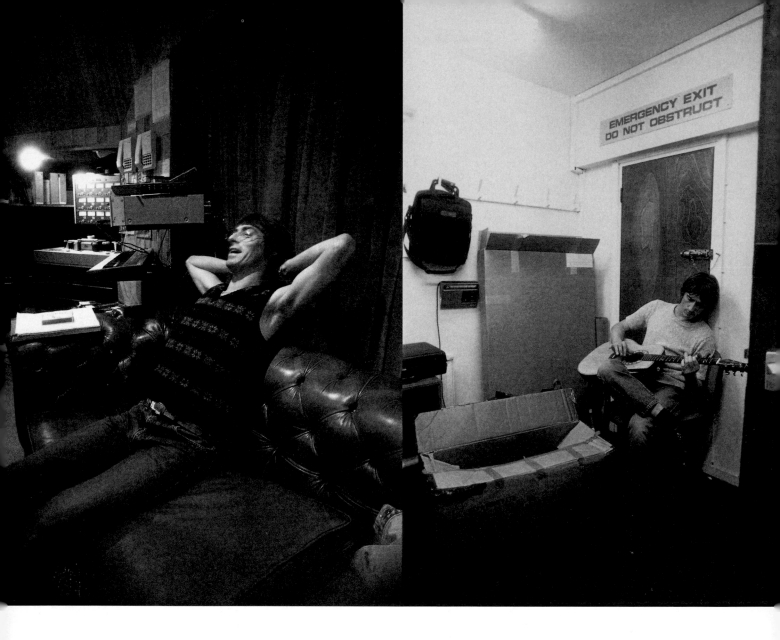

INTO TOMORROW

"I THINK IT'S QUITE AN ORIGINAL SONG AND SOUND. I THINK IT'S ABOUT ME TRYING TO GET A GRIP ON BECOMING A THIRTY SOMETHING AND THE GREAT GREY MASS THAT LIES BETWEEN THE SIMPLE BLACK AND WHITE WORLD OF MY YOUTH."   P.W.

THE FIRST RECORDING OF THIS TOOK PLACE ON THE 25 AND 26 FEBRUARY IN 1991. WE WERE IN THE BACK ROOM AT SOLID BOND STUDIOS (PAUL'S OWN STUDIO AT THE TIME) BECAUSE THE YOUNG DISCIPLES WERE IN THE MAIN STUDIO DOING THEIR ALBUM. WE ACTUALLY GOT SNOWED IN. WE COULDN'T GET OUT SO WE STAYED THERE FOR TWO DAYS. IT WAS GREAT BECAUSE PAUL WAS KIND OF INTO THE IDEA BUT HE WASN'T SURE ABOUT THE SONG. BUT BECAUSE OF THE SNOW HE HAD TO STAY THERE. I KEPT WORKING AWAY ON THE SEQUENCERS AND THE ARRANGEMENT. THERE'S ONE LITTLE BIT IN THE SECOND VERSE WHERE ALL THE DRUMS DROP OUT AND IT ACTUALLY HAPPENED ON THE DEMO. IT WAS A COMPLETE ACCIDENT BECAUSE THE SEQUENCER WAS PLAYING UP. WE HEARD IT AND BOTH OF US SAID THAT'S GREAT, WE'LL HAVE TO USE THAT. SO ON THE FINISHED RECORD THEY DROP OUT FOR A BAR OR TWO. ON THIS I HAD QUITE A FEW IDEAS AND THIS WAS LIKE MY FIRST PRODUCTION. ALL WE HAD WERE SAMPLES AND ABOUT

ALFWAY THROUGH THE DAY HE SAID, "I'VE
OT SOME LYRICS." HE JUST HAD A VERSE.
 LOT OF HIS SONGWRITING AT THAT TIME
AS DONE ON PIANO THAT WE HAD IN THE
AIN CONTROL ROOM BUT THIS ONE WAS
ORE BASED AROUND BEATS AND BASS
NES AND THEN STARTING WITH A MELODY.
 WAS MORE DANCE BASED. WE THOUGHT
HE DEMO WAS GOOD SO WE TRANSFERRED
 TO 24 TRACK AND ASKED THE LATE
REAT JIMMY MILLER TO WORK ON THE
NAL OVERDUBS AND MIX. UNFORTUNATELY,
HAT DIDN'T REALLY WORK OUT. PAUL WAS
EHEARSING FOR THE MOVEMENT TOUR AND
E DECIDED TO TRY CUTTING THE SONG
VE. THAT MADE IT MUCH BETTER. THE
RIGINAL GUITAR SOLO FROM THE EIGHT
RACK WAS USED ON THE FINAL VERSION.

IT WAS BASICALLY HIS GUITAR THROUGH A
LITTLE PINK MARSHALL AMP. IT'S ACTUALLY
A TOY AMP. WE PUT IT IN A FILING CABINET
AND I PUT A MIKE ON IT. IT WAS THE FIRST
SOLO HE PLAYED FOR THE SONG AND IT
WAS THE ONE THAT ENDED UP ON THE
RECORD. EVERY TIME WE TRIED IT AGAIN,
EITHER THE SOUND OR THE PERFORMANCE
WASN'T UP TO IT. IT'S A GREAT SOUND,
REALLY METALLIC. I'LL ALWAYS REMEMBER
WHEN WE FINALLY WENT HOME IN A CAB
AFTER THOSE TWO DAYS. PAUL GOT OUT
OF THE CAB AND HE LOOKED BACK IN AND
SHOOK MY HAND. I COULD JUST TELL
THAT HE'D FOUND IT AGAIN.

BRENDAN LYNCH

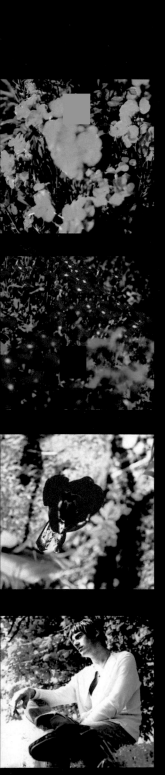

Royal Albert Hall 22 November 1994/*matinee*

We were mixing "Fly On The Wall" at the Hit Factory. Paul was rehearsing at Easy Hire and he popped into hear the mix. While he was at the studio, he asked to put down a quick demo with just acoustic guitar and vocals. He had the whole thing. Music, lyrics and arrangement. The funny thing was that he had been really busy for the last couple of months and I had been working with him, so I never figured out when he wrote it or when he had time to write it. That was on 17 June 1992. The following month we did some demos at Nomis studios and we went through the track again. Paul had been playing it live but he wasn't really happy with it, so we worked out the bass and drum patterns. The next year, when we were recording the "Wild Wood" album, Paul said he'd like to sing it outside because it was that kind of song. We tried it with Paul sitting outside on a bench with a few umbrellas around the mike because it was windy. Unfortunately, it was too noisy. We couldn't use it although it sounded great, really dry. We went inside and got it in one or two takes. When Portishead did their remix of it (for a give-away NME single) they called me up and said, "You've sent us the wrong tape. There's only one vocal and no click track on it." A click track is a metronomic beat that you use to sing along with. I said, "Well, it was live and he just played acoustic guitar and sang." I think it was a new concept for them because they always work with machines and overdubs. I know that Paul is really happy with this one. He thinks it's perfect which is very rare. For all of us.

BRENDAN LYNCH

"I tried to write a folk song, or at least my interpretation of one, a very traditional olde ballad one, where the chords don't change throughout the song and the only changes come from the dynamics of the playing and the lead voice. When we played it in Glasgow last year, the crowd started to sing with us, the whole crowd, and they were so loud it drowned us out. It then felt like "Wild Wood" <u>was</u> a real folk song and that touched me. A real <u>folks</u>' song."   P.W.

Natty Weller, his friend Josh and his father head for the hills, Spring 1993

Paul, Steve and Marco Nelson. Wild Wood sessions, July 1993

*"Every time you think you've got life sussed something else happens.
And there's been quite a few things where I've just realised I know fuck all.
I'm still starting really."*

"Sunflower" — (Takes 3 & 4)

" Can you heal us (Holy man)" (TK. 2)

" Wild wood" (TK. 5)

" Has my fire really gone out?" live a (TK. 2, 3 & 5)

" Moon on your pyjamas" (TK. 15)

" The weaver" (TK. 8)

" 5th Season" (TK. 8 & 9)

" Country" (TK. 4, 5 & 6)

" All the pictures on the wall" (TK. 6 & 7)

" Shadow of the sun" (TK. 8 & 9)

"Kenny has been with us for nearly sixteen years and he's the one who cops the most flak. A tour manager's role is the toughest in my opinion. They get it from all sides, band and crew, and at times from the promoter, manager and punters. He's had near heart attacks over us, me and Papa John, but I love him because he's always looking out for us. I hope he knows that, this grizzly bear with a heart of gold."

"I still have this feeling that my time is yet to come, that I'm going to make something really great one day. Whether I will or not, I don't know. But that's part of what keeps me going."

Tokyo, October 1994

"THE MUSIC IS THE ONLY THING THAT STILL MAKES SENSE TO ME. IT'S A ROCK OF SANITY AMID LIFE'S INSANITY."

Rehearsals, The White Room, 17 April 1995

"I've always waited for the legs to fall out from under me. It's why I've never been be able to enjoy what we all term, 'my success'. I hate using these clichés like, 'success,' 'fame', and 'sex', and 'drugs'. Because they are myths created to hold the masses in suspension and out of the truth. It's the middle-class revolution, creating its own spells to sell to the working class who neither love nor hate you. For most people are indifferent. They've got their own shit to contend with."

Soundcheck, Tokyo, October 1994

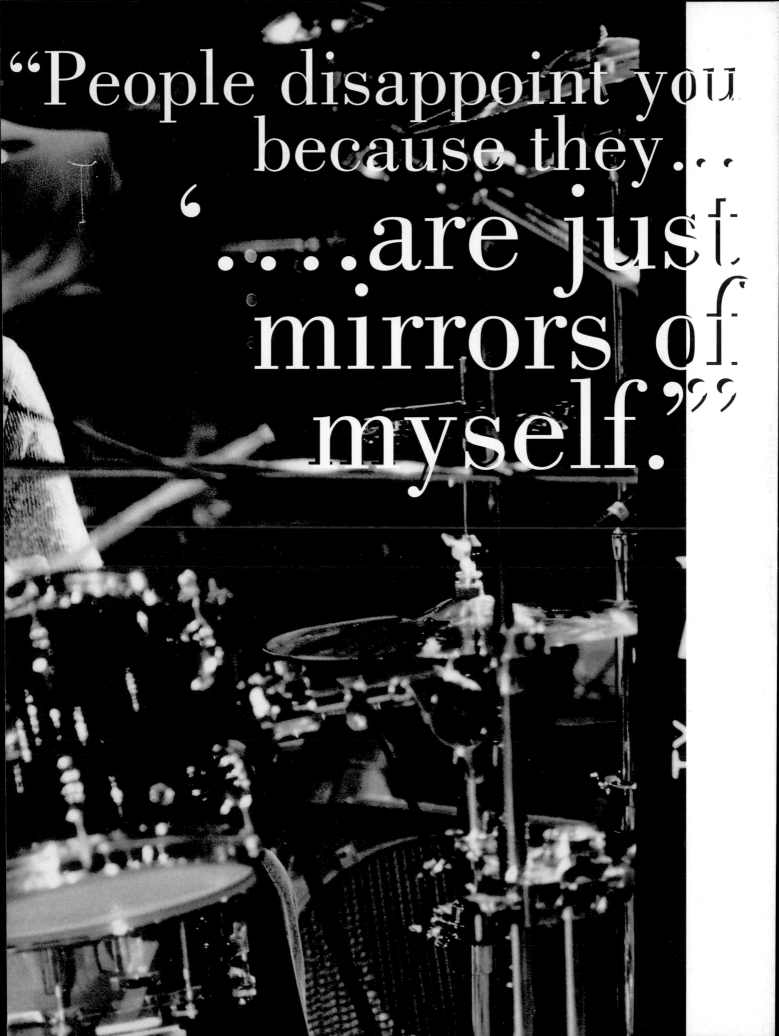

"MAYBE IT'S MY COMPLEXES, BUT I GET THE IMPRESSION THAT MOST PEOPLE DISLIKE ME ANYWAY, SO I ALWAYS START THE CONVERSATION FROM THAT POINT. IT CAN ONLY GET BETTER."

Hamburg Airport, 15 November 1994

yo, October 1994

"WAS IT MY FIRST CIGARETTE OF THE DAY? OR DID I HAVE ONE WHEN I GOT UP? I'M HUNGRY! WE WERE UP AT NINE AND WE'RE OFF TO BRISTOL. IT'S A LONG DRIVE. CHIP SHOP! THE COACH PULLS UP. I GET PIE AND CHIPS BUT I CAN'T EAT AT ALL. IT'S TOO EARLY. LAST NIGHT WAS HAPPENING! WE GOT OFF AND SO DID THE AUDIENCE. WE WERE AT ONE. IT WAS A HIGH. THERE WAS NO WAY I COULD GO TO BED WITH A GOOD BOOK AND A HOT CHOCOLATE. MY HEAD IS BUZZING. IT'S PART EGO, PART ADRENALIN AND, LAST NIGHT AT LEAST, EXPRESSIVE SATISFACTION. WE PULLED IT OFF! THE CROWD WERE WITH US! IT REALLY DID MEAN SOMETHING TO OUR LIVES. AND THERE IS THE DANGER. A DELICATE BALANCE OF BEING MEANINGFUL AND BEING REAL ABOUT IT TOO. THAT'S VERY HARD. SEE, IF THERE'S ONE THING I CAN'T STAND IT'S GOING THROUGH A ROUTINE, THE MOTIONS. I LIKE SPONTANEITY. I ALWAYS HAVE DONE. THAT'S WHY WE TRY TO KEEP THE TOURS DOWN TO 2/3 WEEKS AT A STRETCH."

Dr. Robert Howard, Steve White and Paul. Soundcheck for Joe Awome (RIP)
Benefit gig at Shepherd's Bush Empire, 4 December 1994

John Weller – the true star of the piece. He knocked off lead in the winter of '63. Bad weather called off the building trade so he found other means of survival. He was an all-round athlete, a trainee journalist after leaving school, a man who boxed for England, who won the ABA, to hod carrier to cabby to hustling us gigs, to all this…

"I feel I pale in his shadow, a hard act to follow. Yet it's me who receives the accolades and applause. Hopefully he gets his through me but that I'll never know."

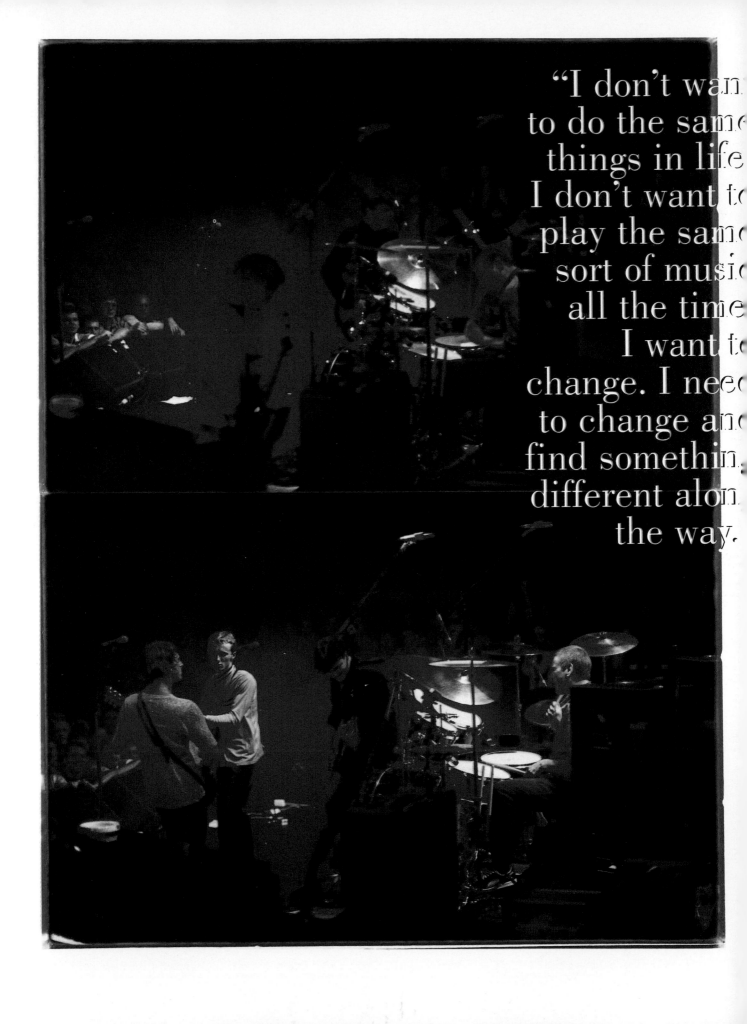

"I don't want to do the same things in life. I don't want to play the same sort of music all the time. I want to change. I need to change and find something different along the way."

Guildford Civic Hall 1994

"IT'S NOT SETTING UP THE TOURS THAT'S THE PROBLEM.
IT'S THE PISS-UPS WHEN YOU GO ON THEM." —
JOHN WELLER AND KENNY WHEELER

Dressing Room, Hiroshima, October 1994

"YOU CAN'T TRUST SUCCESS, IT'S A VERY TRANSIENT THING."

Steve Cradock, Dr. Bob, Paul, Helen Turner and Brendan
Lynch at Radio One Session, Maida Vale, 26 April 1995.

Mick Talbot, Marco Nelson and Paul Weller

IN NOT MORE THAN FIFTY WORDS WRITE DOWN
YOUR CURRENT THOUGHTS ABOUT YOUR TWO
PREVIOUS BANDS.
„I CAN'T REALLY.„
IT'S ALL A DREAM.
WHAT WAS YOUR LAST DREAM ABOUT?
„JUST THAT.„

"I don't believe in politics any more. I don't believe in religion
particularly. But I am hungry to make music. It's like my faith really."

Brendan Lynch, Steve Cradock, Seamus Fenton, and Helen Turner - Radio One Session, Maida Vale, October 1

Marco Nelson and Mick Talbot do the Dormouse.
Clive Sparkman, Paul & Steve stay up past nine

"Someone was asking me about authors the other day and I said to them, 'Lennon and McCartney,' because that's what I was reading at eight years old. It was valid to me then and it still is now."

See, at most gigs, everything is equal but at The Paradiso the odds are always slightly against you. That's because the herb is legal there and by the time the band hits the stage, most of the audience is usually skunked and blunted up and watching the world in a haze. It makes for a real soporific atmosphere. The people aren't "up". They're in a warm daze.

I've seen Paul play his heart out there before and it looked like he was trying to wake the near-dead. So this time around he was ready, more so than he usually is. It was like a grudge match. That's why he asked all those band members who imbibe not to indulge two hours before the show. He wanted everyone fit and on the case.

I'd been playing tunes for about two hours and by the time they hit the stage, you could touch the heavy cloud of smoke that hovered above. Paul wasn't having any of Sometime that day he had determined to get that crowd on its feet, come what may. So when he walked on he looked taut, focused and resolute. Probably, in fact, how his dad must have looked all those years ago when he climbed into that boxing ring and was seconds away from the opening bell.

The band kicked off and right away it was obvious that something was in the air. All of them were playing their hearts out but none more so than Paul. He towered over that audience and he glared at them, looked them straight in the eyes and dared them to refuse his music. He would open his voice and these dramatic words would ring out, sung with a passion that only in his later years he had started to truly locate in himself.

Then he would move away from the mike to prowl the stage, to swagger, his face contorted with meaning and sweat, egging on the others with looks of terrifying anger or incredible bliss. And all the time he was wringing music out of his guitar with a ferocious energy that sometimes belied belief.

The rest of the band kept up with him but it was from Paul that the strength for the night was coming. He was the source and that is what made it so fascinating. Nothing it seemed could stop him. Or could it? That was the marvel of it all, this tension between success and failure.

The music started to cut through the haze. You could actually feel it starting to spread throughout the club everyone started to realise that something very special

It's impossible for me to tell you the best concert I've ever seen Paul give because, especially of late, there have been so many memorable nights. Glastonbury, Manchester, that time at The Albert Hall when the lights came on and all the people were on their feet, Berlin, the list is long. But if I had to pick one it would be his show at The Paradiso Club in Amsterdam on 11 November 1994. I know the date because it was Lawrence Watson's birthday.

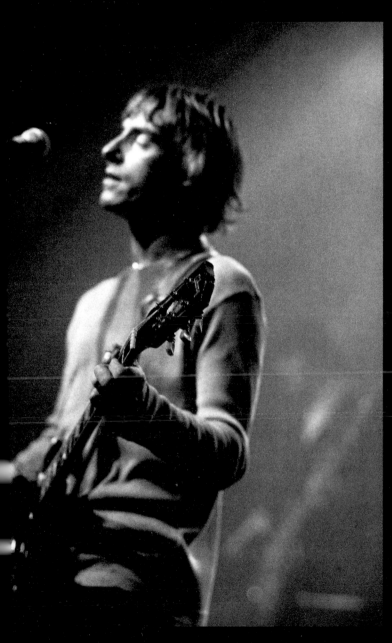

taking place. As each song finished, the crowd start-
to roar that little bit louder and by the time he was
ee quarters of the way through the set, Paul looked
and he knew he had them against the ropes. So what
he and the band do? Coast for victory? No way. They
ed up the effort even more. They had sensed victory
they were not about to back off now. It was then
they put everything they had into it, playing with a
ver and a passion that was coruscating. If the crowd

had been wobbling earlier, they had no choice now. They
gave over. Big time.

I think Paul and the band played three encores that night
and then they were gone, dripping in sweat and smiles.
The lights came up and that was my cue to play a tune
and ease everyone out. But the crowd refused to move.
They stood in front of that empty stage and they
screamed for more. And more. And more. They did this

Paradiso Dressing Room, Amsterdam, 11 November 1994

...r at least ten minutes. Then they did it for another five ...ntil, finally, unbelievably, the band were back on stage, ...learly exhausted but flushed with the excitement of it ...ll, their brains running at about fifty miles a minute.

...Now, if anyone is aware of their work it's Paul, so when ...e launched into "Heatwave," he knew exactly what the ...ritish contingent down the front would be thinking. ...heir heads would be filled with Jam nostalgia. But the ...ight was beyond such feelings. The gig had seen to that. ...aul and his band had wiped the slate clean that night. ...hey had made sure that they and the audience were ...ot at odds. Now the band were the audience and vice ...ersa. Everyone was on the same wavelength and it ...oesn't get much better than that. That night "Heatwave," ...ever sounded better in that man's hands.

...t was an incredible performance, magnificent in its' ...each, heroic even. Everyone on that stage had taken ...hemselves to the limit and then gone ten steps further. ...t was the gig you never wanted to finish. When the ...and finally quit in love and exhaustion, and the audience ...new they could demand no more from them, I turned ...o Alfie the lighting guy who was standing next to me. ...e was wistfully looking at the stage. "I don't know how ...e does it," he said, "I just don't know."

...e being me, I thought to myself, I'm going to find out. ...y the time I had my records together and the hall was ...ow eerily quiet but somehow still buzzing, the band had ...ready left the hotel. I walked over to the hotel, dumped ...y tunes, and went to find them all.

...hey were in Cradock's room, including Paul. Downstairs ...the bar a cute little girl had given me a little bit of an ...ve so I was in something of a hurry to get back there. ...ut first there was some business to attend to. I got a ...rink and went over to Paul and we sat there, supping, ...uietly chatting. Just as I was leaving, I turned to him and ...id, "P. I got to tell you this, that was some performance ...night. Where the fuck did the energy come from? I ...ean, towards the end I really thought you were going ...drop down but you just kept coming and coming at ...em all the time. You never gave an inch."

...ul looked glazed and tired beyond belief. "It's the ...usic," he softly said. "The music just keeps me going." ...odded like I understood but the thing I remember ...e most is the almost sad tinge that was mixed with ...e wonderment in his voice at that moment in time. ...June of 1995 the Dutch magazine OR, voted Paul's ...nsterdam gig the best concert at the Paradiso of 1994.

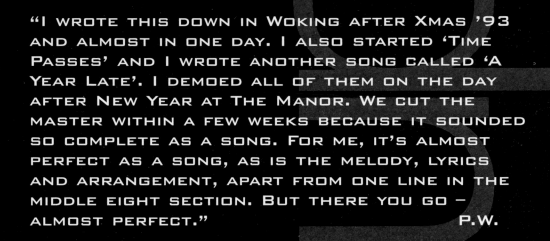

"I WROTE THIS DOWN IN WOKING AFTER XMAS '93 AND ALMOST IN ONE DAY. I ALSO STARTED 'TIME PASSES' AND I WROTE ANOTHER SONG CALLED 'A YEAR LATE'. I DEMOED ALL OF THEM ON THE DAY AFTER NEW YEAR AT THE MANOR. WE CUT THE MASTER WITHIN A FEW WEEKS BECAUSE IT SOUNDED SO COMPLETE AS A SONG. FOR ME, IT'S ALMOST PERFECT AS A SONG, AS IS THE MELODY, LYRICS AND ARRANGEMENT, APART FROM ONE LINE IN THE MIDDLE EIGHT SECTION. BUT THERE YOU GO — ALMOST PERFECT."   P.W.

PAUL DID A DEMO OF THIS AT THE MANOR ROUND XMAS '93. I THINK RIDE WERE IN THERE AND THEY HAD A COUPLE OF DAYS OFF, SO PAUL ASKED IF HE COULD USE THEIR INSTRUMENTS. THEY SAID IT WAS OKAY. HE DID QUITE A FEW DEMOS, THIS BEING ONE OF THEM, JUST ON HIS OWN. I THINK HE ALSO TRIED TO RECORD "YOU DO SOMETHING TO ME" FOR A POSSIBLE SINGLE AND THEN THOUGHT HE'D TRY THIS ONE AS A SINGLE AS WELL. WE REHEARSED IT AT NOMIS AND I WENT IN THERE AND CHANGED A LITTLE BIT OF THE ARRANGEMENT ON THE MIDDLE EIGHT BECAUSE BOTH PAUL AND I THOUGHT IT WASN'T WORKING. EVEN SO, IT WAS PRETTY MUCH ALL THERE. IN FEBRUARY, WE WENT INTO THE MANOR FOR THREE DAYS AND PUT IT ALL DOWN WITH THE BAND PLAYING LIVE. SIMON FOWLER FROM OCEAN COLOUR SCENE DID SOME BACKING VOCALS IN THE MIDDLE EIGHT. PERSONALLY, I THINK THIS COULD HAVE SOUNDED BETTER. THINGS AREN'T THAT CLEAR ON IT BUT IT DOES HAVE A GREAT ENERGY ABOUT IT. ON THE RECORD I THINK IT'S JUST A LITTLE BIT TOO SLOW. THEY DID A VERSION OF IT AT THE BBC FOR AN EMMA FREUD SESSION AND IT WAS A LOT FASTER. THAT COMES ABOUT THROUGH PLAYING IT IN. IF WE HAD LEFT IT FOR A COUPLE OF MONTHS AND LET THEM PLAY IT IN, IT COULD HAVE BEEN BETTER AS COULD THE PRODUCTION. THE FUNNY THING IS THAT A LOT OF PEOPLE SAY TO ME THAT "HUNG UP" IS A GREAT TRACK AND THEY LOVE THE GUITAR SOLO BECAUSE IT'S SO LOUD. MAYBE I'M BEING TOO PERFECTIONIST ABOUT IT. SOMETIMES YOU GET IT REALLY PERFECT BUT NOT OFTEN.

BRENDAN LYNCH

Metropole, Berlin 13 November 1994

Paradiso Club, Amsterdam, 11 November 1994

AMIDST ALL THE WORRY AND CONFUSION WHEN YOU LOST THE PLOT IN THE LATE '80s, WHAT IS THE ONE THING THAT YOU HAVE DETERMINED NEVER TO GO THROUGH AGAIN?

"COMPLETE SELF DESTRUCTION OF MY CONFIDENCE."

Shepherd's Bush Empire, 4 December 1994

Metropole, Berlin, 13 November 1994

"Steve Cradock, has given me and us as musicians so much enthusiasm, energy, *and* grown in the space of just over a year into a fucking good guitarist who will also just get better and better."

"Steve White's playing is eternal. It's very, very special. He's unique. Sometimes he'll be more inspired than other times but even then he's breathtaking. There's times I've played with Whitey that have been so intense, so frightening because you enter uncharted waters that you couldn't even dream of."

I was away (as usual) on Natty's sixth birthday. We had started another U.S. tour but I got to play "Moon On Your Pyjamas" on the same day, live on New York radio. It's sentimental, yes, but I was trying to send out signals to my son, messages.

Black Barn, September 1993

Hung Up video shoot

OUT OF THE SINKING

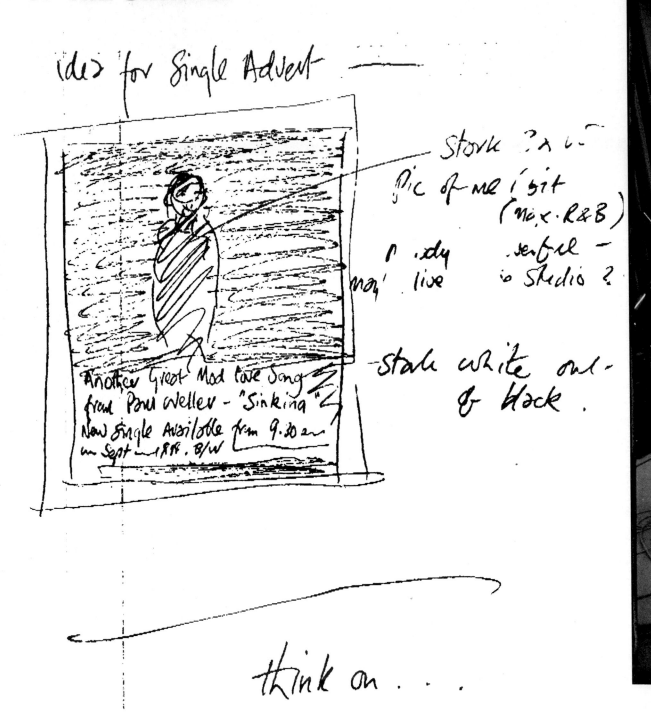

ides for Single Advert —

Another great Mod love Song
from Paul Weller - "Sinking"
New Single Available from 9.30am
on Sept —18th. B/W

Stork ? x vi
Pic of me i bit
(mo,x·R&B)
may' live io Studio ?

-stark white onl-
& black.

think on . . . .

"I WANTED TO WRITE A GREAT ENGLISH MOD LOVE SONG AND THIS IS IT. HOW DID I FEEL WHEN I WROTE THIS? FRIGHTENED, INSECURE, CRAZY BUT POWERFUL. IT STILL MAKES MY BACK TINGLE WHEN I HEAR IT. IT STILL FRIGHTENS ME BUT IN A WONDERFUL WAY THAT I HOPE I CAN NEVER EXPLAIN. THE MIDDLE SECTION IS PURE SMALL FACES AND PROUD, AND THE LINE 'ACROSS THE WATER' IS THE THAMES."   P.W.

WE FIRST CUT THIS IN APRIL OF '94. PAU
SOME ROUGH IDEAS AND WHEN WE WERE
TRIDENT DOING "INDIAN VIBES" (A TRACK
VIRGIN FRANCE THAT PAUL PLAYED SITAR
PAUL ASKED TO PUT DOWN SOME DEMOS
INCLUDING "TIME PASSES". AT THE TIME
SONG HAD A VERY BASIC STRUCTURE, NC
RHYTHM, JUST GUITAR AND VOCALS AND
VERY ROUGH ARRANGEMENT. WHEN IT CA
THE BASS LINE, HE STARTED PLAYING IT
WAY BUT I SUGGESTED A STYLE WHICH W
MORE LIKE THE BASS LINE FROM FLEETW

"ALBATROSS". HE PLAYED IT THAT WAY
A FAR MORE RIGID STYLE. THE NEXT TIME
D THE SONG WAS AT GLASTONBURY.
STANDING NEXT TO JOHN WELLER AND
5T TURNED TO ME AND SAID, "NEXT
I HEARD IT AGAIN AT THE PHOENIX
AL AND THE NEXT DAY WE WENT DOWN
MANOR AND PUT DOWN THE FIRST
OF SONGS FOR THE "STANLEY ROAD"
THIS WAS THE SECOND SONG WE
DED. THE FIRST WAS "STANLEY ROAD"
HE OTHERS WERE "TIME PASSES", "SEXY

SADIE", "WHIRLPOOL'S END" AND "YOU DO
SOMETHING TO ME". ALL OF THEM WERE
DONE IN TWO WEEKS. "SINKING" WAS A HARD
TRACK TO RECORD BECAUSE IT HAS SO MANY
DIFFERENT PARTS AND SECTIONS WHICH ARE
ALL LINKED BUT HAVE TO HAVE THE SAME
POWER OR FEEL. YOU GO FROM THE GENTLE
INTRO TO THE REALLY POWERFUL CHORUSES
AND I REALLY THINK THAT PAUL'S PERFOR-
MANCE ON THIS IS OUTSTANDING.

BRENDAN LYNCH

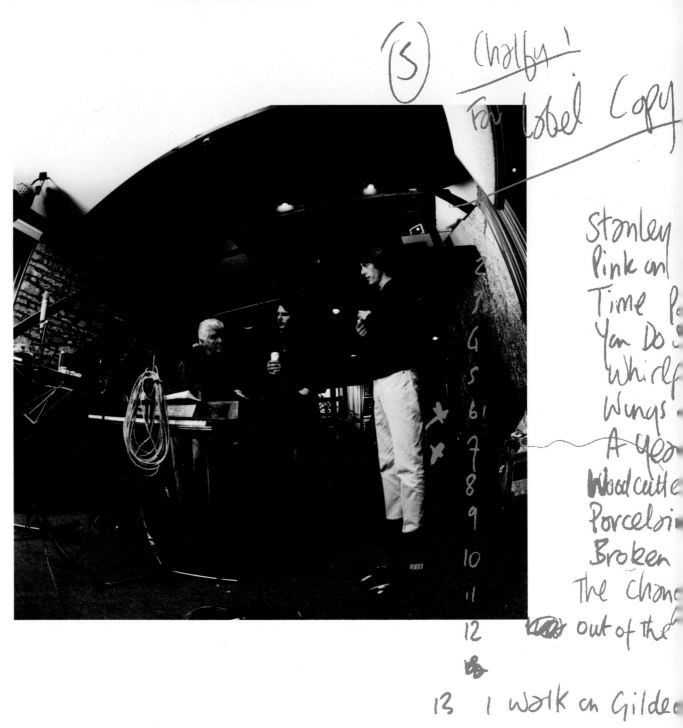

"On 'Wings Of Speed' I tried to describe the feelings I get from 'The Lady Of Shallot' by John Waterhouse which hangs in a bad spot in the Tate Gallery in London. Check it out. It's still free! I'm no art buff – I like what I like, etc. – but the lady in the painting looks real, she looks like she could step out of it at any moment. And the anguish in her face. The painting moves me and I don't really know why. I just enjoy it. I tried to make the song part Afro-American gospel and part English hymn."   P.W.

HEN FAME OPENS HER MOUTH, YOU HEAR…
OOK OUT MUSH, TROUBLE!'"

a t'other –

PORCELAIN GODS

"THIS IS ME PLAYING LOTS OF ROLES, PHONEY ICON TO ICONOCLAST. THE LYRICS ARE INTENSE AND DRAMATIC. I WANTED A SENSE OF OVERBEARANCE, AN EDGE BETWEEN SANITY AND ALMOST LOSING IT, HEADY, AND IT'S ALL THOSE THINGS TO ME. I REALLY CAUGHT IT IN THE LYRICS AND IN OUR PLAYING ON THE TRACK. THE OUTCOME, I SUPPOSE, IS, LIKE IN A LOT OF MY SONGS, THAT IN THE END YOU HAVE TO BELIEVE IN YOURSELF. THE 'MORE EMPTY WORDS' ARE THE PROPHETS, SEERS AND SAGES, WHOEVER YOU LIKE, AND SOME OF IT IS ABOUT ME AND DEE. 'TOO MUCH WILL KILL YOU, TOO LITTLE AIN'T ENOUGH.' A FEW PEOPLE HAVE ASKED ME IF IT IS ABOUT GEAR BUT I MEANT IT TO BE ABOUT SUCCESS AND FAME. IT APPLIES TO MOST THINGS I SUPPOSE. APART FROM LOVE, MAYBE."   P.W.

PAUL HAD BEEN JAMMING IDEAS AT SOUNDCHECKS DURING HIS LAST TOUR AND WE PUT DOWN A VERSION AT THE MANOR ON 19 JANUARY. PAUL DIDN'T REALLY HAVE A MELODY STRUCTURE OR LYRICS – AT LEAST I HADN'T HEARD THEM AT THIS STAGE. WE HAD A BREAK FROM THE ALBUM ON THE WEEK STARTING THE 30TH JANUARY AND ON THE THURSDAY OF THAT WEEK, WE WORKED ON THE TRACK AT THE DEMO ROOM IN THE SOLID BOND OFFICES IN NOMIS STUDIOS. I TRANSFERRED THE MANOR VERSION TO MY EIGHT TRACK AND PAUL SANG THE SONG FOR THE FIRST TIME – BRILLIANT! THE NEXT WEEK, WE RECORDED SIX TAKES AND USED THE LAST TAKE. WE HAD TO CHANGE THE LENGTH OF THE SONG TO FIT IN ALL THE LYRICS. SOMETIMES, PAUL WILL START WITH THE LYRICS, GET A MELODY AND THEN WORK OUT THE INSTRUMENTATION UNDERNEATH. OTHER TIMES, HE'LL COME IN AND PUT SOMETHING DOWN. LIKE "BULL-RUSH". HE CAME IN AND PLAYED THAT ON ACOUSTIC GUITAR AND I THOUGHT IT SOUNDED GREAT LIKE THAT. BUT HE SAID, "NO, I WANT TO DO IT WITH THE BAND", AND IT WAS EVEN BETTER. SO THERE AREN'T ANY RULES. SOME TRACKS ARE OBVIOUSLY GOING TO GO ONE WAY AND ON OTHERS YOU BUILD ON THE BASIC IDEA. ON THIS OCCASION, PAUL STARTED OFF WITH A BACKING TRACK OF RHYTHM, BASS, DRUMS AND GUITARS, AND IT DEVELOPED FROM THERE. AT THE END OF IT, I SAID, "CARRY ON, GO INTO ANOTHER BIT", AND THAT'S THE JAM AT THE END OF THE TRACK WHICH IS NICE.

BRENDAN LYNCH

"When I'm on stage, it's almost like there's only one thing that matters: to prove my music, to prove myself."

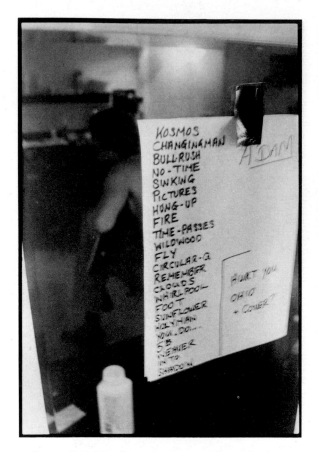

y'know. Check most roadies. Just give them a few sherbets and encouragement and they'll chat the hind legs off a donkey. They'll tell you where you are going wrong in your career, who's right in the band, who's not, how to play your guitar, sing properly, you fucking name it. Perhaps it's a case of music and all its peripheral parts attracting 'big' characters or at least characters that are full of themselves."

"Inside the business side of playing music, you'll see many a struggle and tussle of egos and it's interesting stuff. For the people who work in it, apart from those playing instruments, writing songs, etc., it can be frustration or a mixture of admiration, maybe jealousy or envy. It's only human nature. That's why you'll find so many 'larger-than-life' characters in the music business, from roadies (probably top of the list for thwarted/frustrated egos), to A&R <u>men</u> who have their fingers on the 'pulse' but mainly on their dicks, to tour managers, secretaries, wives, friends, fiends… all sorts,

John and Ann Weller with former security man, Joe Awome. May he rest in peace

Mr David Liddle, strangely quiet. Paris, November 1993

Steve, Noel Gallagher and the changingman

Paul, Helen, Marco and Michelle Howard light the fuse

Find
musical
value & chord-hook } G6/A

Broken Stones

1. Like pebbles on a beach
   Kicked around, displaced by feet
   Like Broken Stones
   All trying to get home — trying to get home

2. Like 2 losers reach
   Too slow & small to hit the peaks
   Oh So, (like broken stones) lost & alone
   Trying to get home — (like Broken stones)

'Br/ch'. As more pieces shatter —
   & get pulled away — & get blown away —
   ~~Something~~ Another bit-/piece (lost) — more pieces (little bits)
   At such a Cost I Can't afford — lost along the way —

☆ is there a pattern in the mess? ☆

   A piece is pulled away —
   Another bit= shatters
   more —(Another) piece's lost (along the way)
   At such a Cost ~ Such a Cost —

   Outside my door
   the oceans roar — melts into thunder —
such a powerful force
So powerful a force — We're cast asunder

Key A (or Bb)

V — A (E /Dᴬ / B7 — E7
   " " " " A —
Br — Dᴬ /A /8ᵗʰ'ⁿ /G6 — Abᴵᴵ — Aᴮ

ides - A or Bb -

Atlantic/Aretha
vibe - Gospel
funk

Broken in beaten by rain
   & storm, fear & hate,
love & war
Smashed to stone's by
the weight of life
(Like Broken Stones — etc —)

What do you think about the most ?
"Writing."

Noel Gallagher and Our Paul rehearse "Talk Tonight"
White Room, 17 April 1995

Bataclan, Paris, 10 November 1994

Messrs. Blake, Weller & Halfon, 4 December 1994

maybe use as
Poster / Flyer / Ads
etc—

Add "The" —

Full title is —
"The changingman"

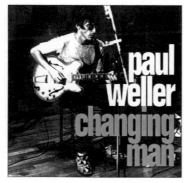

let's go f
one — PW

change "m
+ add "The"
"changing

Full Title is —
"The changin

Changingman sleeve ideas

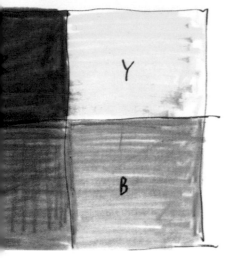

Y

B

The Changingman.

appiness real?
m i so jaded,
ut see or feel – like a man ...

... ed by the effect – aware of the muse
i touch with myself – i light the fuse!

e ... the changingman ...
he changingman – waiting for the long – ...

is on loan – only and to borrow
i ... today, i ... be tomorrow
the more i see ... the more i know
more i know – the less ...

a bigger part –
our instincts ...
t in the dark –
... ment in black –

the more i see – the more i know.
more i know – the less i understand –

"I would hope that this LP represents a significant change in me and my music. I've reached the bottom at times whilst also soaring to fantastic peaks (Glastonbury '94) and they both seem like scales out of control. I've tried to put some of those feelings into these songs."

WHEN THEY COME TO GET ME

And when they come to get me,
When they come…
Who will look after my children?
Who will be there to love and protect my wife?
Who will save them from the savages of war?

Will I ever see again
The green hills of my homelands?
The smiles upon my babies' faces
The blue skies of summer?
The kiss from my wife's sweet lips?
When they come to get me,
When they come.

If they come to get me,
Will I be strong?
Stick to my vow that it's better to die
Than be shamed?
The vows we all may say
But who's to know,
If they come to get me.

LARSON! LARSON!

My name is Larson! Larson!
I'm as hard as nails,
Walk down the High Street,
Scratching my arse,
I don't give a fuck,
And why should I?
I'll fight any bastard who catches my eye.

Our old man drank,
'Til he couldn't think,
He came home later,
And beat the shit out of his kids,
In the daytime, our mum was on sleepers,
At night she was on her back,
She turned to brassing,
When our old man went down,
And I remember every face,
Who passed thru' our front door,
We'd lay awake in our bedroom,
As she faked another groan,
Fucked another punter,
We got breakfast on our own,
(And put on dirty jumpers, we never had a home).

My name is Larson! Larson!
And I don't give a fuck,
I'm as hard as nails, I am,
And I hate everyone.

I grew up in a world that hated me,
And so I hate the world.

My name is Larson! Larson!
I'll fucking glass you,
I'll walk down the High Street,
Scratching my arse, I don't give a fuck.

LAMBRETTA LOVE POEM

My SX is gleaming bright/white,
Take a ride with me tonight,
We'll fly to the stars that never were,
Before tonight, just glimmers, tiny candles,
In our minds (burning bright in our minds),
Wish upon, wish upon.

Get dressed up and we'll be gone,
Out of the smoke and city shriek,
Into something far more deep,
And with a sweet whisper in your ear,
I'll take you away,
And start to steer into bliss, upon your kiss,
And together we'll stay, forever this way,
Locked in ecstasy, lost in emotion.

You're my ice cream girl,
You always will be,
I lap you up,
You make me weak,
I'll melt your heart,
With a quick kick start.

My SX is gleaming bright,
Take a ride with me tonight.

TWO UNFINISHED

There's a stillness in the air
And the grass crackles under our feet,
The sun is big and hanging like an orange disc,
Deep, deep in the sky,
Clouds appear at our mouths,
As we breathe and we breathe and sigh.

Happiness fleeting – a transient thing,
Comes in many colours,
Clothes itself in silk,
Smiles like a golden woman,
Raising you by dawn (so warm)
Raising you with warmth,
And you love every moment,
Unprepared for dawn,
Whatever you get – you must give back.

Stillness in Lions Cemetry.

- FallsRd -

~~(scribbled out)~~

She lost her life
a tragic bullet
strayed but strategic
    killed her in an instant
~~(scribbled out line)~~

Her ma was passing
As she was hit
She saw her go down
Her angel face on the dirty ground
A Mother's only daughter
Caught in crossfire slaughter

The child she carried
in her swollen belly
The angel child in a mothers eyes
~~(scribbled out)~~

(Who) watched her grow
& prayed to God
to spare her life
& mine to take
Watched her fall
    in any Falls Road
        in any folks town

how
ed shot her down   (devils)
an angel face on the dirty ground
A Mothers only daughter
Caught in crossfire slaughter

O If all we had we're in our hands
We'd carry mountains to other lands
We'd skim across the earth on melted butter
Sail across a Sea of Milk
The bones of others, rattlin' behind us —
Crying out — please set us free,
                please set us free.

~~FallsRoad~~ ~~Falls Town~~ ~~Falls Road~~
As if by magic we would change
Or nurse the sick an carry the lame
Metaphorically — hypothetically
It's all bullshit to them —
While some still try - to justify,
The dying too must wonder...
        Why am I not living.

If all our Sins we could put right
And tip imbalance over night
Would the whole world choke its own rapture
Finally part of the final chapter—
In the beginning there was the Word
But words aren't enough - to save the world
        To save the world,

Em / +add melody/RIFF All was my cornfields.
E/G/B/G-A-
Am —   Am6   x 2
I was on a high ~
Though I'd killed my time. ~~was wasted~~
Before I took a dive - as i recall -
Before the fall ~
        All was my cornfields.

I was on a climb
that maat said stop
But is it a crime?   Em/Em/Am/
When your heart leads you   Am/B m+
                                C Bm+

■■■■ :   Same change?

i was on a high
the dressing room humming
i played all i wanted to say —
& everyone was buzzing
The World was right,
Right at that time
I looked at her & she at him
I took another puff
- the geek kicked in.

Bdim.
Chords Em4 D/G - to open / Em D/F# - G - to open -
Am   F#-G x 2
Em etc /

i was full of shit
& i had it - raining
i felt it all a lie
& i (was) wanting
    nothing -

gman video shoot, April 1995

PAUL'S TOP FIVE'
PAUL WELLER SOLO SONGS
AS OF MAY 1995. (NO ORDER)

PORCELAIN GODS
WILD WOOD
INTO TOMORROW
OUT OF THE SINKING
AND
YOU DO SOMETHING TO ME

TOP FIVE SOLO
PAUL WELLER SONGS
AS VOTED BY
A CAST OF TWENTY-THREE.

1. BROKEN STONES
2. WILD WOOD
3. TIME PASSES
4. SHADOW OF THE SUN
5. YOU DO SOMETHING TO ME

VOTES TAKEN FROM: PAOLO HEWITT,
SIMON HALFON, STEVE CRADOCK,
STEVE WHITE, MARCO NELSON, JOHN WELLER,
ANN WELLER, DAVE LIDDLE, MIKE HENEGHAN,
TONY CREAN, PEDRO ROHMANYI,
JEFF BARRETT, BRENDAN LYNCH,
NOEL GALLAGHER, DAVID LODGE,
ANDY MACDONALD, DR. ROBERT,
PIPPA HALL, SEAMUS FENTON, JOHN REED,
DODGE ASPINALL, ANDREW JONES
AND ALFREDO ZAMMIT.

GO! Discs and **Paul Weller** have compiled a free CD of previously unreleased material available only to those who have purchased *Days Lose Their Names and Time Slips Away*. The CD contains the following tracks, all demo recordings from the Stanley Rd sessions:

STANLEY ROAD
PORCELAIN GODS
TIME PASSES . . .
BROKEN STONES
YOU DO SOMETHING TO ME

To receive your free CD please carefully cut out the coupon on the corner of this page (photocopies not accepted) and send it with a cheque or postal order to cover postage and packaging (see below), to:

Paul Weller CD Offer
Trinity Street
3 Alveston Street
Leamington Spa
CV32 4SN

Postage and Packing
United Kingdom £1.00
Mainland Europe £1.50
Rest of the World £2.00

Please rush a FREE Paul Weller CD to:

Name
Address

Post Code

I have enclosed a cheque/postal order for
£1 _____ £1.50 _____ £2.00 _____ (please tick)
payable to "Trinity Street"